Urban Legends

Urban Legends, Volume 1

Tobias Gray

Published by Tobias Gray, 2023.

To my family, who terrify me more than anything.

To my favorite person, you inspire me to keep plugging away at this...thank you.

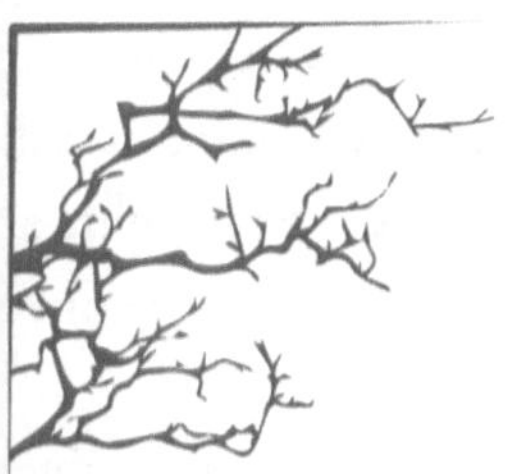

Camping

My friends and I decided that we were going to go camping in the woods. Our parents were against the idea but we managed to wear them down after a while of begging. We drove there in my older friend's car, we thought we had brought everything that we needed to stay for the weekend. Extra clothes, an emergency flare gun, and portable battery packs for our phones which were only going to use in emergencies. It was going to be a great trip. The weather was predicted to be perfect and the refreshing waters called to our souls.

When we were scouting out the location where we wanted to go camping, we wanted to pick someplace close to the water that way we could spend our days splashing around and fishing. But the issue was that we were certain that other people would have the same plan, so we made sure that we found a place that seemed pretty unpopular. We weren't worried about animals or bugs, necessarily. We just didn't want to spend our weekend annoyed by the presence of other humans.

It felt like we were never going to agree on the perfect spot until, quite by accident, we stumbled across a location called Seymour's Grange. The reviews were...okay, it was nothing to write home about from what we could see on the pictures but for a small group of friends just looking to make memories for the summer it seemed harmless enough. Plus, it was only about

20 minutes from our hometown, which seemed to help put our parents at ease. I was pretty sure that my mom was going to call the cops and have them drive by our campsite every night, at least she seemed to be thinking about it as the weeks wore on. I think my dad managed to convince her to leave us be.

"They're just kids, Diane, let them have their fun while they can. They won't get into too much trouble. Besides, if they don't check in with us at least once a day, they won't be allowed to do it again, this close? We could drive out there and check on them ourselves."

That seemed to be the last thing needed to get our weekend approved. So, after double-checking everything and assuring our parents that we would check in at least once per day, if not more, and an embarrassing round of hugs that seemed a little too tight, we headed off on our grand teenage adventure.

"Oh, this place is going to be rough for sure," my friend, Karl said, as we took in the beach and the wooded lots surrounding it. The beach wasn't well maintained, and the water seemed clean but just a little bit more stagnant than we were hoping for. Small, gentle ripples gave us hope that we would at least be able to catch some fish, but probably nothing awesome.

"Stop moping and help us get the tent set up," Andrew groaned, lugging a huge armful of camping gear to the spot we had chosen to set up our camp and dropped it with a huff. Every group of friends always seemed to have the muscle and he was ours. He had a career already planned out for the military and we were expecting that he would probably do just fine there. I was more bookish, and they joked that I would probably die in the town's only library, either as a patron or as a librarian.

The first day we spent wandering around and getting familiar with our scenery. It was actually kind of beautiful in that 'forgotten' sort of way. That while it wasn't the place people plastered all over their Instagram accounts that it still held a lot of natural charm and overall felt very...peaceful. Nothing at all like some of the reviews led us to believe. Some of those people must have been paranoid about their experience here.

We ate a modest dinner and set up our tents. It was actually, a really quiet night. As full dark fell over the land we were all amazed and just how...quiet it was. Even for a place that was near the main road, we didn't hear hardly any traffic. It was just us sitting around telling stories, being the book nerd of the group everyone expected me to come up with the best ones. I did my best but I could tell that they lacked a sort of realism that could only come from actually experiencing the strange things that happen to people out in the wild. I guess I was just mostly happy that I didn't have anything crazy to talk about. After all, nobody liked being scared senseless, and while I tried to weave a few entertaining tales I could tell my friends found them predictable.

The moon was incredibly bright and high in the sky as we all finally gave in and went into our separate tents to pass out. It had been a full day and we were ready for some sleep. While we have gone camping, we usually always ended up at crowded campgrounds that had staff that went around making sure nobody was up to anything nefarious or unpleasant. I imagine that those employees might have some interesting tales to tell if we ever asked.

The moonlight, filtered through my tent window was bright enough to read by. I found myself drifting off and unable to focus on the pages of my book. I closed it and just lay there, slowly drifting off to sleep and enjoying the natural sounds of the night. The branches of the trees painted beautiful and slightly hypnotic patterns on the tent.

At some point, I must have dreamt something weird. I...read a lot, okay? I know that gives me a bit more of a hyperactive imagination than most people, but I also tend to have very realistic dreams. So, this was most likely a dream and not something brought on by the books I've been reading, I had even been taking a break from the young adult horror category and have been trying to read things that are a bit more mysterious lately. This was just so weird. I dreamt that I was lying sort of awake in the tent, not entirely awake yet. I heard something very gently, very softly caressing the outside of the tent.

I snapped awake, in full terror, thinking that some wild animal was trying to push its way into my tent, I could only make out a thin, vaguely humanoid shadow retreating away from my tent. Those assholes! They were trying to scare me into thinking that something was trying to rip its way into my tent. I peered through the netted window of the tent and as far as I could see in the strange bone-white gloom of the middle of the night was...nothing. There was nobody there. I didn't even hear them try to get back into their tents several feet away from my own. I would have almost been impressed if they hadn't managed to scare the absolute hell out of me.

After deciding that I would confront them for it in the morning and several hours of silent fuming, I managed to drift back off to an uneasy sleep. I was certain it was one of their pranks trying to get under my skin but at the same time, I couldn't shake the strange feeling that I had seen a glimpse of something otherwordly in that shadow on my tent. It was probably just my sleepy brain playing tricks on me.

I was the last one out of my tent in the morning, nobody seemed to say anything about it, which annoyed me. According to the watch I brought with me for timekeeping, it was already 10:30. Today we were planning to go hiking around the area and see if there was anything cool to take pictures of. Karl was going to be going to college next year for photography so he always relished the chances to take pictures of places we ended up. It was sort of nice, having our photographer in the group. Otherwise, most of our memories would probably just evaporate with time.

We ate a quick breakfast and I forgot how much I enjoyed cooking on the campfire. Everything just tastes so much better, even if it was just some simple breakfast burritos. We made sure that we grabbed fresh water from our car and then double-checked all of our gear and made sure that we weren't likely to get bit by anything on our ankles and off we went. It was a beautiful day for hiking and we had a lot of fun trying to identify all of the plant and animal species that we could remember.

Eventually, our path lead us back to the campsite but from a different angle. We were able to take some good pictures of the small lake and we made plans to double-check for anything unpleasant in the water before we went for a swim later. I wished we had brought a kayak or some other small boat so we could have just lazily drifted across to the other side. My attention was torn away from the lake by a question Andrew asked.

"What do you think made these tracks? I've never seen anything like them."

Curious, I came around to see what he was talking about. About a hundred yards away from our campsite in the damp mud that was already drying in the midday heat, there was a series of thin prints. The impressions weren't great but whatever it was seemed to be bipedal and very thin. Almost, as if a skeleton had been walking past us in the night. I briefly thought about my dream but I didn't want to say anything, last thing these guys needed was another reason to pick on the nerd. I shook my head and stepped away from the marks.

"No idea," I said. "They might not even be animal, they aren't very deep and it could have been from any number of things. I don't recognize them, anyway."

Karl took a photograph of them and we went on with our day. We spent the afternoon cooling off in the lake, which seemed fine if in need of some maintenance work. They probably didn't do much with the park as a whole since it probably didn't see enough traffic to justify the expense. I wouldn't blame them for that. It's not like parks and recreation get a good deal of budgeting anyway. As the day wore down we decided it was time to engage in that time-honored tradition of making s'mores on the campfire and once again we engaged in telling twisted tales. I told them about my dream but in the guise of a camper that had gotten lost in the woods and experienced the strange nocturnal visit from The Thin Man in his sleep.

"Holy shit, dude, that's messed up," Andrew remarked, laughing nervously. "That was a really good one. I'm proud of you. I need you to write that one down for me, so I can tell it to my nephews."

Karl looked around at the darkness, I noticed that his attention kept slipping in the direction of the strange thin tracks and he seemed distracted. When it was his time to tell the scary stories he just waved it off and said that he had enough and it was time for sleep. I had been getting drowsy from the activity of the day and lulled by the heat of the fire, so I agreed, I wondered if they would try to prank me again or if I had just really dreamt it. I figured after telling my Thin Man story they would have realized I was onto them. At least, I hoped it was them I was onto.

Once again I felt myself falling asleep while reading, I laid back on the pillows and let the soothing sounds of night carry me off to sleep. I was jolted awake by a sudden sound. I lay there, in confusion trying to decide if I had just dreamt it or if there was something outside of my tent. The sound came again, this time it was like someone had been running their fingers across the surface of the tent. I froze, my blood turning to ice in my veins.

Mixed in the ever-shifting shadows of the tree branches against the tent there was a sudden but inexplicable motion. A movement. I scurried to the back of my tent, as far away from the window and door as I could. I could see the shadow move along the wall of the tent. Did it pause? As if considering, thinking, maybe it was even listening? On the wall of my tent was a single thin hand pressed against the fabric. The material was straining against it, and whatever was pressing in was bone-thin. I stifled a scream by biting my finger. I must have bit myself hard enough to draw blood as a rich copper taste filled my mouth.

"What the fuck is that?" I heard someone whisper. The shadowy figure's weight suddenly departed the tent, and it was just gone. I shook like a leaf in the wind. A moment later, there was the sound of the zipper at the entrance of my tent. My relief when it was just my friends was palpable. I nearly cried.

"I thought it was something trying to get into my tent, was it just you guys fucking around?" I asked, through shaky breaths. They all shook their heads, and I could tell from their solemn and wide-eyed expressions that it wasn't them. They saw it too. I asked them to tell me what they saw.

"I had to wizz, so I crawled out of my tent and that's when I saw it standing by yours, I couldn't see much, it was like...light wouldn't touch it. It made my eyes hurt to stare at it. But man, that's the horrible part. I couldn't see its face but I knew, I just knew that it was watching you sleep inside the tent. Like...I got the impression that it was...hungry," Karl said, his voice cracking on the last sentence.

None of us slept a wink that night, and nobody really questioned why we wanted to come home early from our camping trip. They seemed to think we were all too embarrassed to admit that we had gotten homesick, but that wasn't the case. I still don't know what we had run into in the woods. I still don't know what it wants from us...from me. Sometimes I see a shape on my window in the early morning dew, it fades quickly, but for a mere moment, there was a bone-thin hand-print on the glass.

Overnight Shopping Trip

I know that I am in the minority here, but I'm grateful that the last few years have brought about the end of a trend that I'd only ever had bad experiences from. The late-night shopping trip. I was grateful for the convenience and the quiet was enjoyable but this one time at a major retailer had changed this experience for me entirely. At least under this strange new way of life we've all been hit with I know, nobody else has had to go through what I did.

I was going to a major Michigan university, studying premed. I hadn't really decided what I wanted to do next, but as the semester was coming to an end I had all summer to think about it. The end of the semester always brought an unwanted guest. End of semester tests, reports, and labs. I felt like I hadn't had a day off in weeks. Naturally, if this stress wasn't enough I found myself in the middle of a more extreme than usual menstrual cycle. Fucking, wonderful.

It was getting pretty late one night and I had been swamped with work (Part-time at the Ice Cream Barn) and school and realized that I was running out of supplies and I was starving and needed some good food. Knowing that I wouldn't have time tomorrow, I opted to go that night and take advantage of the overnight hours. Quick in, out, and I'd still be in bed at a fairly reasonable time. With a sigh, I parked my car in the nearly deserted parking lot and made my way inside.

Anyone who has ever been in a large retailer in the middle of the night probably knows what a surreal feeling it is. It is a strange emptiness that seems to give you a very strong feeling that you're not supposed to be there. That a place that is so accustomed to loud, unending crowds becomes something otherwordly and sacred when the stillness of night comes.

Even the workers seemed to be afraid to break this sacred silence. They were going about their overnight stocking and cleaning tasks with only making the bare minimum of sound necessary. They even wore headphones and avoided idle conversation. That might have also had to do with the fact that the overnight manager was notoriously ruthless about hitting their objectives. Or at least that's the way all of her classmates who had tried moonlighting at the retailer had made it sound.

She had to admit that they were doing a really good job pulling the place back together from the chaos of the day. Everything seemed way more orderly and easily navigable than it had whenever I visited throughout the day. I was finding that my shopping was going way smoother than I had expected. I had found almost everything on my entire list in what felt like record time. I didn't even have to stop and bother any of the workers.

I finished my shopping on the merchandise side of the store and then headed back to the grocery side of the building. Since I hadn't needed much and certainly couldn't afford any of the electronics. This side of the building felt older and the numerous superficial remodels weren't very effective at covering it all up.

I picked out the usual bunch of sweets that I couldn't ever seem to go without, I also managed to pick up more coffee. I was worried that my coffee habit was going to be the end of me, but it was at this point the only thing that was getting me through the never-ending slough of coursework that I seemed to always be suffering under.

As I wheeled my shopping cart down the canned vegetable aisle the light overhead flickered. With a high-pitched buzzing noise, it went out. I wasn't worried. The building wouldn't be pitch black because of a couple of burned-out bulbs. I would just tell the cashier on the way out. As I wheeled to another aisle a different light above me went out. Thinking maybe there was an electrical problem, I moved out into the main aisle way.

I was staring up at it wondering if I shouldn't flag down one of the workers. Maybe it was something that they were working on, after all, I've seen several maintenance men carrying ladders back and forth around the facility. I decided that I should probably tell someone because this probably wasn't normal.

Before I had seen several employees working in different parts of the store but as I wandered the aisles I didn't see any of them. It was almost like they had all decided to go to their breaks at the same time. It figures that something weird would happen when they did that. I made my way to the front of the store.

As I did, more and more of the lights started to go out above me. As I ran up to the front of the store the lights kept going out, following my path and tracing a line of burned-out bulbs across the high ceiling. Some of them were going out with such force that the glass was shattering. I finally saw the back of an employee ahead of me.

I grabbed ahold of the man even as the lights above me flickered and started to go out. I turned him around to ask him for help or at least to explain what the hell was going on and when he made contact with me, his eyes turned into pools of darkness. Black ichor began to run down his face as his mouth twisted into an unnatural grin.

"How may I help you?" he asked.

I stumbled back, trying to get away from him. He never stopped grinning even as he reached toward me. The look on his face was troubling me, but the lights above us kept going out and I wasn't going to get trapped with this...monster in the dark. I took off down a different aisle, my cart forgotten.

I dodged several more employees, all of whom had the same look on their faces and the same dark sludge oozing from their eyes. They seemed to be just...wandering. They didn't seem violent, but I didn't give them a chance to get ahold of me. I had to get the hell out of there. I made it up to the front of the store but to my horror, there were several of the creatures – because there was no way these were real humans – standing in front of the door surrounding the manager.

"Leaving so soon? You haven't even completed your purchase. Tsk, tsk, we can't have that," he said, his voice a raspy whisper. If the workers found him funny, they didn't react. I certainly didn't find him funny.

"Like hell, this isn't happening." By now I was convinced that I was in some sort of nightmare and that the only way to break free of this nonsense was to just exit the building. I even tried to pinch myself. It didn't work, and the manager didn't seem to show any interest in letting me leave the store peacefully.

I hoped that these employees were just as slow as the rest of them. The lights had been steadily burning out and were getting close to the front of the store. The rest of the store appeared to have been swallowed by the approaching darkness. I couldn't even see the lights from the cooler and freezer section. I wasn't going back that way. I took a deep breath and rushed to the employees at the front.

"No! Stop her!" the manager screamed, waving his arms at me frantically. The movement seemed to get the employees moving faster, but they were still too uncoordinated to catch up to me and I was outside of the building. I stopped for a moment to catch my breath and ease my burning lungs, I turned to see if they were chasing me.

The last thing I saw was the darkness falling over the front part of the store. The manager stared at me from within, his eyes burning into me. The light above him went out and I couldn't see him anymore. I got into my car and peeled the hell out of there.

I wanted to file a police report but what would I tell them? Would they believe me? I tried finding the place the next day, thinking maybe I had just imagined the whole thing and perhaps I owed someone an apology. I couldn't find the building for hours, I was on the verge of giving up when I found it again.

There was no signage on the outside of the building and there weren't any cars in the parking lot. I approached the outside of the building which said 'for lease' in the window in on a badly made hand-written sign. I looked into the building as deeply as I could. There was nothing but a thick layer of dust.

I still don't think anyone ever believes me when I tell them this story. In fact, I have had several people ask me if I have ever been on drugs but I haven't. I was completely sober. One day I hope to figure out exactly what happened but I am afraid to go looking.

The Hopping Horror

Everyone always says, tell us your scariest story. The thing that happened to you that nobody else is likely to believe. The problem is that all of these years later I'm still not entirely sure if I even believe what happened to me. It didn't help that I've spent all of these intervening years trying to find some way to cope with the trauma. I have turned to both therapy and uh, recreational...substances...trying to find relief but I swear, I can hear those horrid sounds every time it gets quiet. At least I have Spotify now.

Okay, I know that you're all going to laugh at me. Call me crazy, tell me to stop doing so many drugs, I've heard all the jokes before. Now that I've had time to process I would almost understand why someone would find it so damn funny. However, for me, it's not very funny at all.

So, when I tell this story please do me a favor and try to put yourself in my shoes. After all, what I'm asking for here isn't anything too difficult, I just want you to understand that for me at that moment regardless of whatever I was experiencing I was afraid and this fear still haunts me to this day. I wonder if I would be able to ever revisit this place in my life without feeling like the end was brought nearer each time I retell it...

I was a young adult, barely in my 20s. I was learning pretty quickly that growing up poor made it difficult to break free of poverty's gravity but even if I had to work half a dozen jobs I was going to get ahead. I refused to be like my mother had become before the disease took her, sullen, defeated, and full of misery that she was quick to inflict upon others. Heart disease is another wonderful family curse. I'd find a way to beat that too if I had to.

Breaking generational curses wasn't my only past-time however, I found myself working so many odd little jobs. Some of them would only last for a few weeks and then I'd be shuttled off to the next one. For an economy that seems to always be struggling to fill experienced workers, they sure seemed hesitant to let you develop enough experience at any one job for long. A friend of mine likes to tell me that this is so they can pay less including hiring costs than the costs of raises and promotions for excelling employees. Ah well, what can you do?

One of the many jobs I took was as a part-time security guard for a company that renovated old buildings into apartment complexes. We worked in teams of two, they didn't give a shit what we did as long as we did our checks. I found myself working on that novel I always wanted to write. That was something of a secret project of mine. Don't tell anyone, shh. Maybe that's the real reason I find myself moving jobs so often, I'm just filling time and trying to pay my bills while I work on the writing thing.

This job started up in around, July. Mostly just covering shifts at vacant, half-finished construction sites. The risky nature of exploring these places seemed to keep a lot of the trouble away. I would only have to call the police for a couple of drinks here and there. One time a suspected overdose, but really, the jobs were pretty gravy. As the construction projects neared completion they would transition us to other project sites.

My least favorite of these project sites was probably the most involving construction project that we had been a part of. They were tearing a building down to its foundations and then rebuilding it into one of their most ambitious apartment complexes yet. It was going to be a huge thing with an indoor gym and pool, among other things. The job seemed to be lasting forever, it was nearly October by the time that we were stationed there full time.

It was freezing at night and by the time they started having some structure built, we finally had a small shack installed for us to work out of. It was barely a shelter against the elements and we never bothered to be as thorough with our sweeps of the place as the bosses would have liked but we figured that if anyone wanted to freeze their asses off to mess around in a half-finished building, they deserved whatever frostbite they ended up with.

By Oct 14th, they had managed to build a good portion of the building. It now had some completed office areas, and a mostly finished roof, but still felt very empty and alien. My co-worker and I had just finished our rounds and I found myself talking the poor guy's ear off about my novel. I had hit a big part and I was hoping that he would be able to give me feedback and inspiration. He didn't have a clue what I was babbling about.

"Look, I'm just saying that I don't know if I should charge forward with the murder scene or if I need a little more time for the emotional impact to build, getting the reader to know a bit more about the characters, you know, what they want to achieve in life. That's when you do them in, really sells the pain." I felt like I was doing a really good job selling the methodology I was using to pace my novel.

My co-worker to his credit didn't seem to just brush me off. if anything, he just looked like he wanted just to go back to sleep. We were halfway back to the closet that served as our office when we heard the sound. It was one of those things, where you think you hear something so you stop and listen, and for a second you have this like...fear, in the pit of your stomach that nobody will ever believe that you heard something.

My coworker stopped and listened to me, he looked at me like I was going crazy. He let out a deep sigh and motioned for me to move on. I laughed a little bit, I guess I was just hearing things then. He looked a little bit spooked himself, but he was probably just trying to keep up a brave face. He always had to be the macho guy of the group.

Later on in the evening, we had to do another round. This time we were both maybe just a bit spooked but mostly tired and wanting the night to be over with already, so we could go to bed ourselves. We had made it about halfway through our tour when we realized that one of the partially built offices had a door that was now open, that was odd because we didn't note any opened doors on our previous tour. My coworker knocked on the door.

"Security! We're coming in, if you have any identification, have it ready." he nodded to me to take the backup position, if something happened I was to immediately relocate and communicate. Since he was the senior guard and I was very new I hadn't been put through firearms training yet, knowing that he had his firearm ready gave me some measure of comfort.

He shined his light in through the room and then nodded to himself before closing the door. They noted it on their report as "Unlocked office door, left ajar. Undiscovered on the previous tour." They didn't find anything else in their tour worth noting on the way back through the building.

Once again, near the shack that served as our temporary base, I heard it again. A distinct sound this time. He paused because he had heard it too. It was a sound that was hard to describe at first. Like, a thick, wet, unpleasant sound. A cartoonish "plop" that seemed to echo unnaturally around us.

Once again a sound like a wet -plop- and this time we realized that it was also very regular. Like, something was moving towards us with one gruesome plop sound at a time. "What the fuck is that?" My co-worker asked. I honestly have no good answer for him. There was something more to this. I felt a peculiar fear. It was...primal. I was convinced that there would soon be a perfectly rational explanation and yet every fiber of my being screamed for me to run. That the thing that was coming around the corner would only ever exist to do me harm and that I needed to just get the hell away from it.

After several painfully long moments, the damned thing *hopped* into view. It stood about three feet tall. It had no discernible body but was instead a horrid single eye fixed to a raw and bleeding stalk of muscle that ended in a single taloned claw. The claw seemed to be leaking viscous black ooze and was the source of that vile sound that accompanied that awful locomotion. Plop, plop, plop. My co-worker reached for his gun but an eye-wrenching beam of red light was emitted from the creature and struck my co-worker who turned into stone right where he stood, without a proper support structure his body fell, rigidly to the floor.

I wasted no time in my mad scramble to get away from the horrible thing. I don't know if it couldn't keep up with me or not but I wasn't about to waste the time to find out. The police were incredulous at first as I wheezed my story into the phone in my locked car. They agreed to send someone out to investigate.

It felt like an eternity, each passing second I was convinced that the thing I had encountered would find me out here in the parking lot. Finally, the soft and blinding blue/red lights of a squad car pulled into the parking lot, I gave them my information and a quick recant of the situation and with their weapons drawn, the police and I reentered the building. They told me I should wait outside but I told them that I didn't feel safe out there alone. I must have been spooked because they didn't argue with me after that.

We found my coworker exactly where I left him, one of the offices phoned in it, and the other began questioning me since this did look for all the world like a murder. You see, I don't know what happened after I left the body but something must-have. Not only was his body still rigidly petrified, but now one of his eyes was missing. I subjected myself to a full search and complied with the entire investigation, eventually, they were convinced of my innocence and I was released.

Naturally, the thing didn't show up on the camera so despite my protests that there was something there nobody seemed to listen and the construction project moved forward. I was horrified that nobody seemed to care about my coworker's death, but life kept moving and I needed the income. For a long time, I avoided that location by swapping shifts or making excuses but my luck ran out. I'm writing all of this in hopes that maybe someone will finally listen to me, that someone will look into this matter more seriously. Because I hear that horrible, gut-wrenching sound again. This time, there are two of them.

The Infestation

I hate the housing market in my area. There were fewer and fewer respectable places to live and yet the number of shady, under-maintained, way overpriced complexes remained the same. I found myself yet again evicted so I had to suck it up and apply to get an apartment in one such establishment. It would feel like hell on earth but at least I would have a place to go, in a couple of months I might be able to move on.

I kept careful records so that whenever I was evicted I could prove that it wasn't for a non-payment. Despite all of my struggles I always made sure that the rent was paid, whenever I could I would even pay it in advance. What kept happening was that they wouldn't be able to raise the rent on me, so they'd kick me out for some technical reason or another and then would charge the next renter more.

It was a well-known 'secret' that the same family owned the majority of the apartment complexes in the area. They did some fancy paperwork to make sure that it would be legal, but it was probably unethical. When there was always someone willing to pay, it just kept the cycle alive.

After a frantic night of searching listings while staying at my sister's place, I managed to find a location with an opening. I filled out the online application and settled into a long weekend of wondering if I would be able to have a place of my own again soon. I love my sister, but we do not live together well and this is a fact that has only been made sharper by the passing of time.

Much to my, I suppose, relief, I was accepted and had the luxury of staying at the GOldenrod Estates, this isn't the complex's real name, I figured when posting this online I should at least change that much. I was hoping that they've improved from the last few comments that had been left about them. I wasn't feeling very hopeful.

At least it was a roof if barely that. I didn't have time to schedule a proper tour of the place so I found myself just signing the digital agreement and loading up what I could into my sister's van and driving over to pick up the keys. I lugged my things up to the second floor. I let out a groan when I saw the place. It looked outdated and smelled even worse. I was already looking forward to moving out. At least there was a couch, lumpy and moth bitten it was a place to sleep. The thin carpet appeared more soiled than anything.

There was a 'welcome' packet that gave me the complex's by-laws and expectations of the tenets. It also informed me that there would be a cleaning crew coming along to polish the place up, but they had been delayed by an urgent matter. For now, I would be welcome to make myself as comfortable as I could and we would be able to address any lingering concerns after the cleaning crew came.

I scoffed at the nearly empty apartment. I know some cleaning crews are incredibly capable but I wasn't aware of any in the area that would be best described as a miracle worker. I guess I'd have to wait and see how much they would be able to accomplish.

The bed was missing half of its frame, so I dragged the mattress to the floor. Fortunately, it didn't look too bad, just aged and more than a little uncomfortable. It would do, for now, it was important to me to make sure that I only ever viewed this situation as temporary, I wanted to keep moving forward and I wasn't going to accomplish that sitting around moaning about the situation.

I stretched out on the bed and after fighting with the pillow arrangement a few times I managed to fall into a fitful sleep. I felt like I tossed and turned. I dug at the itchy material in my sleep, and my skin seemed to burn where the mattress touched me. I don't know how I managed it, but eventually, I fell into a proper sleep.

I woke up with a stiff neck. I truly slept wrong on the makeshift bed. I dreaded the thought of work but I also didn't want to lose my apartment before I had a chance to obtain another. Somehow, I made it through the day. I was beyond ready to call it a night. I don't even think I was awake for a whole ten minutes before I fell asleep. I was just so drained.

Yet again, I had a rough night of sleep and struggle. This time I felt certain that there was something wrong with the mattress. Like, whatever it was that was causing me this discomfort had decided that it liked snacking on me and came back for more. Bed bugs? I wasn't sure. I thought perhaps I would have seen evidence of them and even with the stiff neck that I still seemed to have, I didn't see any when I craned around as best I could to inspect. I just needed to get a better bed.

The next day I had to call off work sick. There was just no way that I would be able to work. Not only was my neck so stiff that breathing hurt but I seemed to be developing some kind of irritating lumps on the sides of my neck. Great, just what my broke ass needed, medical debt. Reluctantly I decided to go see the doctor. They couldn't get me in until the next morning, so I took the over-the-counter anti-inflammatory they recommended and tried to keep comfortable. Other than my neck I felt fine. I hoped that this wasn't the beginning of something lifelong and severe.

The discomfort was causing me exhaustion. I just kept falling asleep all afternoon. I found the couch to be more bearable than the bed, even if my already irritated skin was grumbling at the rough and unpleasant sensation that the fabric that covered the couch gave me. After a long nap, I felt much better than I had been. I wasn't sure but I felt like the bumps were even receding. I got comfortable on the couch and even watched some television, something I hadn't felt like doing in forever.

I must have fallen asleep at some point. I didn't think I was that tired after all of my nappings but when I woke up, I felt so much better. I felt the best that I ever had. I canceled my appointment and then went to work. My co-workers wanted to know where this newfound sense of energy came from and the best I could tell them was a good night's sleep was all I needed. That night I was taking out the trash when I realized that the world felt very different to me somehow.

It felt like my senses had been somehow cranked up to a whole new level. Like, you know how they talk about people that lose a limb or a sense and find their other senses are somehow sharper? That's how I felt. I don't know what I lost, but I felt like I had gained something. I smiled to myself, my whole life was going to be better from here on out. This would be my rock bottom. Nowhere else to go but up.

I knew I needed to get my work done and get back inside, but the cool night was parted by a sudden breeze that made my hair stand up. My burning senses told me that despite this overall 'wonderful' feeling that radiated from the core of me that there was something else...something dreadfully wrong with everything. I couldn't put my finger on it, but it felt like I was just out of sight of something unpleasant.

The cloud cover parted and when I saw the moon I became transfixed. I felt like I was just seeing it for the first time. And, a new...instinct welled up inside of me. Strange and alien at first but soon felt like the most real sensation that I have ever felt in my entire life. I needed to hum, deep and loud. A rumble that seemed to radiate from my very bones.

This feeling became a mounting pressure that seemed to well up from within me. It was like my head was pounding in time with the universe. It didn't feel painful or stressful, instead, I would only be able to describe it as freeing. Yes, that's what I was feeling. I was finally feeling free somehow.

"What the fuck is that?" My coworker yelled. I turned, confused, what did he mean? He was yelling and looking at me as he ran. I caught sight of my reflection in a puddle of water that seemed to always be by our industrial-sized dumpster. A massive insectoid head with dripping mandibles looked back at me. I ran for my life.

It didn't take long for me to realize that I could never go back to my previous life. I don't know what happened or why this had happened to me. Was it that feeling in my apartment? Is this what happened to the previous tenant? I wish I knew, but I don't know. I just know that it happened to me and I was forever changed, I was continuing to change. I had developed wings now. It was fascinating. It didn't hurt, it felt more like I was shedding something unnecessary. Like clipping an overgrown fingernail.

I went into hiding, I found myself in a nice quiet warehouse that didn't seem to be used and decided to write this so maybe someone, somewhere will know what happened to me. Because even as I write this my...humanity...fades...

The Terror in The Pit

I grew up in a small town in Michigan that if you heard about it, it was because you lived there. Near this small town of mine was another, slightly larger town. This town didn't have much more than ours did but they did have a neat little park that had a place to swim. This place was called The Pit. Originally, it was some sort of rock quarry or something. But supposedly they hit a water table and the whole thing flooded out, they lost all of their equipment down there. Others say that it was intentional and they had everything removed already. Nobody could ever agree on which was the truth.

There were a lot of weird rumors about The Pit and at the age of 17 I was still at an age that I could have willingly believed most of them. We were all at an odd age anyway, we were looking forward to college and the careers we wanted to pursue and developing relationships and all of the drama that went along with that. But still, my little group of pals and I always managed to have a good time.

As we realized that all of our plans would send us in different directions we decided that we were going to need to have one more private party before we separated. I made it clear that we needed to keep the wild and illegal parts of it manageable because I wasn't going to spend my senior year grounded just because we smoked all of Kyle's weed again. We decided that we would see if The Pit was haunted at night as everyone says.

If nothing else it would be a fun memory to look back on later in life. Kyle was bringing his best weed, Alexis was going to steal a few of her dad's beers. He wouldn't miss them, he hardly ever drank the ones he had. It was going to be wild. All we had to do was sneak out of our respective houses and get together at Jake's and take his car. I think our parents knew that we were up to something, but figured we were just plotting a senior prank and that it would be harmless and juvenile. It was a cool night. We had hit that transitional period where summer starts to feel more like fall. It was foggy and the air smelled like that earthy spice smell of fallen leaves. It was the perfect night for some teenage debauchery.

I was the second to arrive at Jake's. Kyle had gotten there first since his parents were never home. Alexis showed up. The only one that wasn't there was Max, but he wasn't one for late-night parties. Deciding that this was going to be it, we loaded up in Jake's car and drove off into the night. We didn't see a soul on our way to the park. We were feeling confident that we weren't going to get into trouble. We parked the car in a public parking area, and then made our way to the park. It would be easier to hide from the police without the car.

Man, we thought we were so smart. I wish we had been smarter. We ate cold pizza and smoked weed and panicked about every little sound. It was so much fun. Then, Jake had the best idea ever. Why didn't we go for a late-night swim? Nobody had to get naked, just slip into the water for one last swim. Everyone must have been feeling the same sort of fading nostalgia because they all agreed that it would be fun. Stoned out of my mind,

I decided that I wasn't going to go very deep, I didn't think I would be able to swim very well until my head cleared, so I just sort of lazily floated around while the others dived and chased each other underwater. They sure looked like they were having a lot of fun. As my head began to clear, so did the night sky. It had been mostly cloudy, the moonlight was bright and we all felt ourselves begin to relax.

As we got tired we decided we didn't want anyone to drown so we took a break from swimming and decided to dry ourselves off as best we could and put on our warmer layers. I regretted that we weren't able to have a bonfire or something, that would have been nice. But I also knew that we weren't supposed to be here either and that if we were playing with fire the police would show up and we'd probably be in a lot more trouble. As we sprawled around the grassy patches near the sandy lakefront Jake asked us if we knew about all of the rumors about the Pit. "Of course we did, Jake, we're not stupid," I told him. He looked a little bit nervous.

Did he know something we didn't know? After some pressuring, he finally relented and said that he would tell us about the kid that got mangled by something here. He said the story goes that a bunch of kids was playing here one afternoon, and they got caught up in these steel lines that run the length of the old quarry. They got sliced up pretty bad. They lived but it just confirmed that nobody knew what was down there and that scared a lot of people. He said he got curious and started asking his dad, who worked construction in the area if he knew a lot about these rumors and whether or not it was likely that there was equipment left down there. He said his dad went to the kitchen and got a beer, drank the whole thing, and opened another one before sitting him down at the table. He's never seen his dad look this spooked.

"Man, I wish I had a beer before I go through all of this again," he said with a weary sigh. He must have been hoping that someone else had heard whatever it was he wanted to bring up, but when nobody else started talking he relented and began his tale. A well-grounded realist he wasn't known to embellish or make things up. After the events that night I wasn't able to sleep so I wrote it all down as best as I could remember, I feel like it will forever be ingrained in my memory.

Jake's dad had been employed as a construction apprentice during the 80s when the quarry was still active. He didn't work there much but just for a few weeks to get some training on the equipment that was conveniently located there. He said the men that worked there were...odd. Like they were on edge. Something had left them unsettled and they didn't' want to talk about it. His trainer was nice, but also seemed nervous and was talking about how he couldn't wait for the current section of their project to be finished because he would be transferring to something else at the end of it. He couldn't wait to be gone.

My dad wondered if it was just the hard work in the heat that was getting them, but despite their scheduled work needing them there until seven or eight, most of the guys were just leaving without approval by like four or four-thirty. He and his trainer had to finish teaching him how to use a rather large and complex machine so they got stuck there close to dusk one night. The trainer was getting increasingly agitated with Jake's father and even told him that he had enough of this and was going to recommend that they just finish it the next morning, not wanting to extend his training into the weekend, Jake's father told him to just finish up with this machine and they could leave, he didn't understand why the man had seemed so upset.

They finished the training section and shut the machines down and punched them out. Night had begun to fall in earnest as they made their way across the quarry to their vehicles to drive up the ramps and out into the night. They froze when they heard the most inhuman sound. The trainer looked up at the night sky. He said that they don't usually do that unless the moon is out. They heard it again, louder. Jake said that his father described the sound as something that sounded like a strange chittering noise, but it was at an odd frequency. It sent chills down their spines and if it was possible their hair would have stood straight up. Not waiting to see how close...whatever it was, was to them they rushed towards their vehicles and jabbed their keys in, engines roaring to life.

The trainer got to the hewn ramp that would lead them out of the quarry and pealed up it. Jake's father was driving as fast as he dared to without risking going right off the ledge. They had made it halfway out of the quarry when...something low to the ground and long slammed into the trainer's car and slid it nearly to the edge, Jake's father could see the trainer try to adjust the movements of the car to get back onto the path when another of those somethings hit the car with enough force to drive it over the edge.

One of them slammed into the side of the truck Jake's dad was driving, it was heavier than the car and didn't slide as badly and he gunned the engine and got out of the quarry. The police did an investigation as well as the company. They could see where his car slid back down and landed upside down. He would have been badly hurt but they never recovered a body. The truck his dad was driving had a huge dent in the side and there was something caught up in the metal, so they had it tested. The damndest thing was that it didn't match anything they've known. Sometime later when genetics got better technology supposedly someone tested the sample and found that it bore similarities to a lobster, but then the sample went missing. Probably got lost or thrown away nobody has been able to figure out what it was. They said it was part of the reason why it was shut down and filled in, to drown whatever it was down there.

Our little group had fallen silent listening to Jake tell his story and Alexis looked especially freaked out. She told him that she wouldn't be able to go back into the water ever again, and I made a quip about how it's not like she showered as it was, and she threw a rock at me. My joke helped break the tension that was holding us all captive we all laughed and started to gather up our things. After all, it was getting super late and we were all starting to get tired from our fun. The bright moonlight made the water sparkle like diamonds. To think that our friend's dad could have died down there. Jake wouldn't be here either, now that I think about it. As we all took a moment to take in the bright night and sparkling water we saw bubbles rise to the surface. Alexis said she hopes it was a turtle, she likes watching them bob along. We waited just a moment longer and as we turned to leave Alexis said to wait a moment.

We turned to see what she was talking about and the shocked silence was broken by Kyle's whisper: "What the fuck!" The water had turned into a roiling mess. It wasn't hot water, it had felt quite cool when we had been swimming in it. Dark shapes were beginning to break the surface of the water and we all backpedaled to get away from the lake. More and more of these dark horrible shapes began to break the water. They were indistinct in the night but their visible parts looked dark and smooth, gleaming darkly in the moonlight. The churning water approached the shoreline. The dark masses piling out onto the shore, and making such an unusually chittering noise, began hungrily tearing into the sandy beach looking for anything they can snap their sharp jaws around.

We were going to be discovered soon if we didn't do something. "We have to go!" Alexis said, nearly a scream. Her voice carried on the wind and the horde began to blindly tear their way closer to our group. We all ran as hard as we could towards the park exit, they seemed to have caught onto the sounds we were making. We barely made it out of the park, the creatures seemed to lose us and didn't exit the park. We made it to the car and didn't look back until we made it to Jake's house. We all just hid in his garage until dawn when he took us home.

We still don't talk about this and I refuse to swim in anything deeper than a kiddie pool. I tried talking to the parks department about the strange things that happened to us and they told us that they had dredged the lake several times over the years and had never found anything unusual. They did report a high number of missing pets in the area regularly but fortunately, no humans seemed to be missing in connection to The Pit.

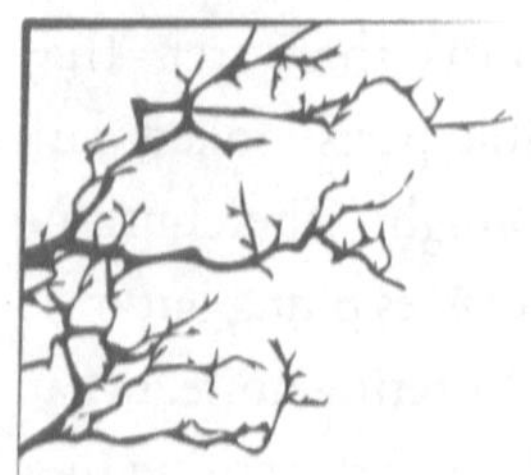

Ruins

I found out that my grandfather passed away one chilly fall afternoon and that he had left the small farm that he had set up during his retirement. It wasn't a huge operation and would probably cost more to update and sell than it would have been worth. So, I decided to take the gamble and see if I could manage it and my day job, I had flexible hours so it seemed like everything was going to work out in my favor. I discovered that the farm was exactly like I remembered it. It was well maintained as even as his health declined my grandfather made sure that the grounds were being maintained.

On my first night at the property, I had a hard time sleeping. I kept feeling like there was...something watching me in the darkness of the old place. At first, I thought I was having a reoccurrence of night terrors, brought on by the stress of my grandfather's passing and the strain of getting used to a new place.

I woke up tired, but it was Sunday, if I was getting anything else done this week I would have to get it done today. I made up a to-do list of things that would be pretty easy to wrap up and got to work on it right after my morning coffee. As I wandered the property and tried to envision what I wanted the place to look like I remember how fascinated I was by my grandfather's simple farming life. I felt that old fascination slowly returning as I explored with new eyes. Not as a child intruding on the life lived by others but rather as someone who was going to shape a new life for himself.

One of the things that struck me as fascinating was that my grandfather's property was far bigger than I would have expected. It included a large clump of forested land that had a lazy river that fed into a larger network of waterways that span the county. I remember my grandparents showed me this place but I was young and didn't realize it was a part of the property. My grandparents showed me it but told me that it was dangerous and we shouldn't play there. There was a section of an underground river that would drag you under and into who knows where. I was an impressionable child and believed them with absolute certainty.

I decided that when I was ready to explore that part of the property I would hire someone to help me landscape it into something safer and more functional. At some point, I would like to have a use for all of the features of the farm, not just the basic crop and livestock locations. I didn't think of it in the vein of profits but rather I enjoyed the challenge. My brother joked that I should turn the place into a petting zoo. Unfortunately, it was far too remote for anyone to want to pay a visit to the place.

I finally got satellite internet set up, it wasn't great but it let me work somewhat remotely, meaning I didn't have to go to work as often. That gave me more time to work on the house in-between projects. I found the work rewarding, if somewhat exhausting.

I was still having the night terrors, too. Now they've evolved to the point that I am almost certain that there is someone else in the room with me until I wake up in a cold sweat completely alone. I had a doctor's appointment made but it would be about a month before I would be able to get in to see the doctor about it.

I had lived there for just under two weeks when I was working on the trellis that would supply support to the grapes that I wanted to add to the farm's already successful berry patch, and I realized that I was close to the section of the farm that had the small plot of forested land. Realizing that I was going to need more water than I had brought with me I figured I could find a safe place to retrieve water from the river head that was there. So a bit apprehensively I took a bucket and a rope out to the river.

The path there was rockier than I remembered. I almost sprained my ankle and made a note that if I was going to use this land more I was going to have to get something done about the paths. My grandfather was a stout man, he didn't have any trouble getting around until his health declined in the last few years. I don't know how he did when I, barely a fraction of his age, was struggling so much with it. I was a sweating, annoyed, and slightly achy mess by the time I made it up the steep path.

I decided that I was going to explore a bit as I hadn't had much chance to look around. The river looked tame enough and I decided I would give it plenty of space anyway, and instead looked around at all of the different plants and rock formations that were left up there. My grandfather must have enjoyed their naturally 'weathered' look because he didn't have them removed, instead might have been planning something like a rock garden at some point. At least, I could put one together if I wanted to now.

The hairs on the back of my neck stood on end. I felt like I was being watched. It was an unpleasant yet familiar sensation and I realized with a sinking feeling in my stomach where I had felt this feeling before. It was the same feeling I got in the middle of the night when my terrors flared up. Whatever was giving me this feeling was the same.

I slowly turned on the spot, but there was nothing there. I was completely alone. I let out a breath that I didn't realize that I had been holding. What was going on around here? I decided that it was probably because I had been alone for so long. I needed to get a dog or a girlfriend. Probably both.

I filled my bucket and went back to my chores. I got the new trellis installed, new grape varieties planted and well-watered. I would need to visit this place every day until the grapes were well established. They seemed to do alright unless we were having an especially dry summer. I went back to the farmhouse to fix myself a hearty dinner before I settled in to read.

I fell asleep that night while reading. I had been reading one of the newest suspense novels. I admit I was up later than I should have been but I had gotten to a good spot and I didn't want to stop reading just yet, but eventually, my tired brain gave up.

Once again I had that sensation of being watched while I was asleep but this time something different happened. Normally, when the terrors hit me, I was lying on my back and facing the bedroom door. However, this time when they took me I was laying on my belly, with my head facing the opposite wall. The lamp painted the room a strange orange color.

A shadow fell across me and to the wall. Whatever was casting it was tall. The shadow moved and I felt a hand gently caress my back and I let out an involuntary sound. The touch was gone and the shadow quietly retreated. Once I overcame my dread and could move again, I was too shaken up to sleep.

When morning finally broke, I had to get to work on my chores before it got too late, and then get to work on my actual job tasks. I wanted to go give the grapes extra water and see how the trellis was holding up. Once again, I decided to just fill my bucket of water from the river.

After filing my bucket I spotted that on the side of the river near me was a hole in the natural rocky wall, what seemed odd was that it looked like man-made bricks on the inside. So, being less brave than I was stupid I decided to crawl my way inside the wall, I was convinced that I would end up finding myself at a dead-end but that didn't seem true as the space opened up in front of me. It was hard to see but I gasped when I realized what I was looking at. There was a living space here, that looked like it had been recently lived in. I got out of there as quickly as I could, leaving my bucket behind.

The place smelled rancid and unclean, but there was a space for sleeping, food containers, and silverware from my grandfather's kitchen scattered everywhere. There was evidence of what I expected was drug use but I had never been adventurous enough to know what any of that looked like outside of movies and television.

I phoned the police and they showed up the next day, so I took them out there and showed them my exact steps but the hole led nowhere. Nothing else to go on, they left and told me to call if I found anything strange. I did my best to not dwell on it. Maybe I had just imagined the whole experience. I was going to move on to my next repair job. But now all of that had been thrown into question. Do you remember that bucket I had left behind? Someone had put it into my locked shed.

Tech Support

What is the weirdest thing that ever happened to me?

I was working late at night at my new apartment. I had a big report due that following Monday and I wasn't going to let my boss down, not after all he did to help me secure this promotion. Unfortunately, my computer wasn't connecting to the work resources I needed so I called the overnight tech help desk. They said it was my internet provider so I called them. They said there did seem to be a problem, others had reported the same type of issues and they were sending a tech out as soon as possible.

I went back to working on the portions of the report that I could access. I figured worst-case scenario I could completely rewrite the whole thing. The lack of internet was starting to get super annoying so I made myself take a break and see if the internet would be working again before too much longer.

An hour passed and I was still having the same problems that I had before. I was on the verge of giving up on the technology and just going to bed. There was a knock on my door. Who the hell? Probably the tech, I figured. A man was standing outside the apartment, he was wearing a blue dingy jumpsuit.

"Can I help you?" I asked him, tired and annoyed.

"I'm the technician that was sent out about the internet issue," he said, looking back, there was something odd about his tone that turned me off, but I just figured he was probably as annoyed to get dragged out here in the middle of the night as I was that he had to be in the first place. It was sort of unusual that he would want to visit me in the middle of the night, but maybe the company figured I was nocturnal and they would save time in the morning.

"Alright, go ahead and come on in." I stepped out of the way so he could enter my apartment.

He was strangely quiet, I tried my usual small talk but he didn't seem to be interested in that, just kept looking around the apartment with a vague curiosity. Something akin to being familiar with something and not sure if he should ask to use it. I figured he was looking for my network equipment and I gestured at the desk where my home computer sat. He nodded and headed over to it and sat down, staring at the screen.

He had begun typing and command boxes were appearing and disappearing on the screen. Lines of code were being executed and he seemed to know what he was doing. He plugged in a USB flash drive and it said files were being copied, I wasn't the most tech-literate person on the planet but since I used that computer for work, I had a lot of questions about what he would need to copy files for.

"What are you copying?" I asked, he half turned to me and smiled.

"There was some malware, uh, viruses, and the like, on your computer system. I am removing them. Don't worry, this sort of thing happens all the time to computers that are always connected to the internet. Your files are perfectly safe."

I wasn't convinced. I didn't know what this man was doing, and now that I thought about it, he didn't introduce himself as someone who worked for the internet service provider either. I was about to ask him who he was again, just so I could call in the morning and confirm when the computer chimed that whatever he was doing was done. He closed everything out and stood up, shaking my hand.

"I've got what I need, thank you for your time, hopefully, that fixes everything but if not go ahead and give us another call and we'll send someone right out," he smiled again, an action that didn't quite reach his eyes. Like he was used to performing social graces but didn't believe in any of them.

The internet was still not working, after a volley of unpolite words I gave up and decided that I was going to just call it a night. I had enough. The internet company was going to get a very loud phone call from me in the morning about their shady technicians who can't even fix a simple problem after they invited themselves into my apartment at three o'clock in the morning.

Around four am after I had been trying somewhat unsuccessfully to sleep there was another knock on my door. Already deciding that tonight was going to be sleepless, I answered the door, ready to yell at someone. It was a man in a clean blue jumpsuit, he flashed me a smile and held up a badge that identified him from the ISP.

He said that he had gotten caught up in traffic and apologized for being so late. That he had to fix a few bad cables outside but found that there were unnecessary cables that seemed to terminate at my apartment's network equipment. He would need to come and take a look to see what's going on. I asked him if it was common for them to send more than one tech a night and he looked at me in confusion as he set up his toolbag by the desk. He was confused, he was the only tech scheduled that night. There wasn't anyone else.

After I explained what the other tech had done, this tech seemed to grow concerned and began to check my computer's activity logs. He seemed to grow more frantic in his typing and started taking down notes on his tablet. I was starting to grow uneasy by how concerned he was starting to become. This didn't seem normal, I was not going to be getting any sleep tonight, thank god it was a weekend. The tech informed me that he would have to call the police and he couldn't find any evidence that I was involved in this.

"Involved in what, exactly?" I asked, incredulous. I was still very much feeling like the victim in all of this. There was no way that I had done anything besides try to get a head on a report that was due on Monday.

"If we're going to investigate this, I don't know how much I can tell you. But I guess, this is your equipment and you – respectfully – don't seem to have a clue as to what I'm talking about, I'll just let you know," he let out a shaky sigh. "There appears to have been...equipment, installed in several apartments. This is the sort of equipment that can get you arrested. Things like voice recorders and cameras. The control software was left behind, but I can see that it must have not have been yours because it was only accessed tonight around the time that you said that this other tech was here."

I was flabbergasted. I was being framed for recording...my neighbors? I sure hoped that they would be able to prove that it wasn't me. I wasn't a fucking creep like that. Man, I was very tired all of a sudden. Like, the air was just let out of me.

"How are we going to prove that it wasn't me?" I asked, "It sure as hell looks like it was me from where I was standing."

"That's why I went through your computer's activity logs. If this was you, you'd probably have been accessing it a lot more frequently. You've never touched it until tonight, I'm sure when we check with the building superintendent you're going to be cleared. But the thing is, this is a felony. So whoever gets caught will have a lot of crimes to own up to. Did you happen to get his name or anything else? What company did he say he worked for?"

I sat down heavily and rubbed my tired eyes. No, I hadn't gotten any of that. I was just hoping to be able to get this report finished by Monday and now I was going to have to talk to the police about this whole situation. I was starting to feel sick to my stomach, but that could have just been exhaustion.

The tech apologized again for the whole affair and said that he would step out and phone this into his headquarters and then call the police, he would recommend that I make myself some coffee because it was starting to look like this was going to be a long night for me. I fumbled my way to the kitchen and realized that I had never seen this mysterious tech before. How had he gotten into my apartment to set this all up? Why would he frame me?

After several more hours of uncomfortable questioning, I was cleared of charges and finally allowed to go to bed. The technician managed to get the internet working again and the building managers changed all of the locks and installed newer security cameras and other things. I was still amazed that nobody have ever managed to figure out not only who had done this, but why. Whatever he had been recording he had deleted off of my computer, so that was helpful for me. As far as I have heard, they've never found the guy.

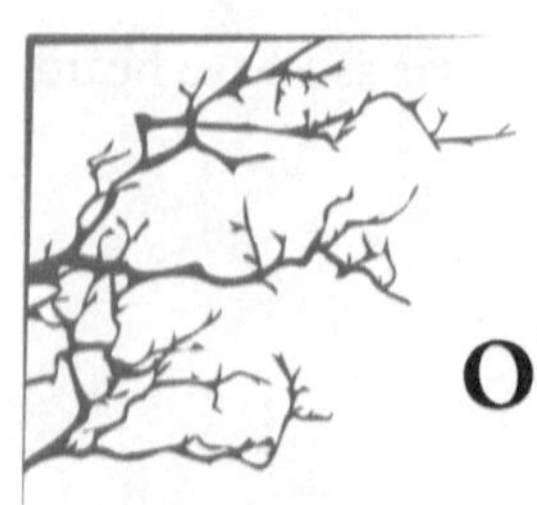

Overnight Stay

My wife wanted me to go along to her 'friendunion', partly to show me off to her less successful friends. She had always had a bit of a chip on her shoulder. She was the last one to find her sense of direction in life so when her goals began to overshadow theirs she couldn't help but get a touch addicted to the feeling of one-upping the others. I shouldn't have encouraged it but I had to admit when she got fired up about something it was kind of hot. So, this along with a few subtle winks and hints towards some adventurous alone time on the trip had me convinced that it might be worthwhile.

After the details were pegged down, they decided that we were going to be staying for five days just outside of Nashville. This would be cheaper than staying IN Nashville. Not wanting to sink a lot of money into a hotel for five nights, we found one of those online short-term rental apps that have become very popular over the last few years. The place had been completely restored just for this purpose and was almost like a private cabin getaway. It was located in a beautiful and rustic lot that was only fifteen minutes from the nearest highway. This meant going to see all of the cool things in the area would be very easy. The price was a bit higher than I was willing to pay, but my wife was in love with the place and I couldn't tell her no. It would give us all plenty of room and privacy and with the location, the girls could be as loud as they wanted to. They were planning on being very, very loud.

I was delighted to learn that I wasn't the only trophy husband dragged along for the trip. It seems like they all got roped into the event. At least I wasn't going to be the only man surrounded by these loud women we have all fallen in love with. The first day was spent exploring the property and we found that the property had a nice clean lake on it and we made plans to hit that up the next day. For dinner, we all drank and grilled and set up various board games that none of us could seem to figure out how to play properly. Despite my initial apprehensions I started to unwind and felt like we were all going to have a pretty good time.

We exchange our best 'dad' jokes and spent the time talking about our shared experiences of being men married to highly ambitious wives. I learned that while our wives were all so highly strung it seemed to open more time for us to develop our hobbies.

"I think it's pretty awesome that we're able to have this, I can't say that there are many men who can enjoy their hobbies so freely. Most of us have to work either just as hard as our wives or even harder. Doesn't leave much room for shenanigans," I said as we drank beers.

"I know right? This is my second marriage. My first one was an absolute nightmare. All I did was work and all she did was spend my money! It was not a good relationship and I'm happy that we managed to split more or less amicably," one of the others said.

I couldn't imagine being married to anyone other than my wife. We had already been through so much. I made a mental note to tell her how grateful I was that I found her first, without having to go through all of the trouble of trying a similar relationship with other people.

That night I awoke around three am and was in dire need of the bathroom. Something I had eaten the night before wasn't sitting very well with me. The bedroom my wife had chosen had a big window view of the wooded lot. The owners had installed some security lights to help ease any fears that their temporary tenets might have about the dark woods. I was still not overly familiar with the layout of the house and was worried that I would open the wrong door to the nearest bathroom. I decided that the next time we have the opportunity to do something like this I wanted to spring for somewhere with private baths.

I finally found the bathroom and relieved my aching bladder. On the way back to bed I paused. Something had tripped the outside light. I was waiting, hoping to see some exotic wild animal but I would have settled for something more common all the same. After not seeing anything for a few minutes, I sat back down on the bed. After a few minutes, the light went out. The sudden darkness was fascinating. After a few moments, my tired alcohol-addled brain startled me. I could have sworn something moved on the edge of the woods.

The next morning I discussed my observations with the others around a heavy breakfast featuring very strong coffee. Almost everyone had a similar experience. It would seem likely then that there was just wild animal out there in the night, curious, and likely tripping the sensors on the lights. We spent the whole day at the lake and the entire experience was a blast. I found myself wondering if I could be friends with other couples like this, I know my wife would be happy that I finally made an effort at being more social. She's already told me that she would like to do this again before much longer.

That night the power flickered and then went out. We had just started our third or maybe fourth hand of rummy and we found ourselves in the dark. we fumbled around and found some flashlights. Outside we heard the sound of crashing wind and thunder. A storm must have caught us unawares and we had no idea how long the power would be out. We moved to the center-of-most room of the building to ride it all out.

We tried to continue our game by flashlight but it wasn't easy and we just decided to give it up. We waited a while by telling each other the scariest stories we had ever heard. They were all the classics. The killer in the back of the car, the man hiding in the storeroom, the killer in the walls. Then we heard a thump upstairs. But we were all accounted for. Must have just been the wind or a branch one of them suggested. I wasn't about to volunteer to go look.

My wife, the brave hero, decided that she was going to go look. They had been drinking some strong margaritas. Her friend, Christy, said that she would go with her. That way she wouldn't be as likely to die, or something else that would have made more sense or been as funny if you were as drunk as they were. They disappeared upstairs and we could hear their steps as they walked across the floors. There was a pause and then a bloodcurdling scream.

We all raced up the stairs, I was taking them two at a time. it sounded like my wife. With the flickering and unsteady flashlight beams, we checked each room in the direction we had heard them going. we found my wife lying on the floor, she was out cold but still alive. Christy was lying on the floor across from her. As her husband reached her body went stiff and rose directly into the air. We all stood transfixed. She opened her eyes and let out a gasp and fell to the floor. Just as her body hit, the lights came back on.

We got them both downstairs and laid out on the couches. We brought them ice from the fridge in the kitchen and tried to get them to come back to their senses. My wife roused first, she was groggy and disorientated and she must have hit her head pretty hard because she was muttering about some girl that they had seen upstairs. But there hadn't been anyone else here...had there? We told her that Christy had the strangest seizure and then she went out cold too. Just like my wife she started to come around a few minutes later, she was just as out of it as my wife had been.

The storm raged on outside. In the lights triggered by the motions, we could see the trees bend and twist. We weren't going anywhere. Just in case they had concussions we told the girls that they weren't going to be allowed to sleep. The other girl went out to the kitchen to get a cup of coffee. When she didn't come back, her husband went to look for her. He didn't come back. It was just the four of us now, I didn't want to worry them but they weren't answering our yells and we weren't about to go looking either. Outside the yard, light began to flicker again.

We were bracing for the power to go out at any second but it was just those lights that were on the fritz. This time however they went out and they stayed out. I could have sworn I saw something move out there, something that was not just a tree branch or something like it. I was about to warn everyone else when something hit the window and I fell backward, over the ottoman. There was another bang against the window and this time something left a wet handprint on the glass. It wasn't a very large one.

There was a gurgling sound and the other guy that was with us hit his knees, blood pouring out of his torn neck, slowly dying the white soft carpet a sticky crimson. The girls were still struggling to make sense of all of this when the lights flickered outside again. For just a brief moment, there were hundreds of figures out there, beyond the edge of the light, shifting and moving, gesturing frantically towards the house. Then, the lights went out. My god... they're inside the house!

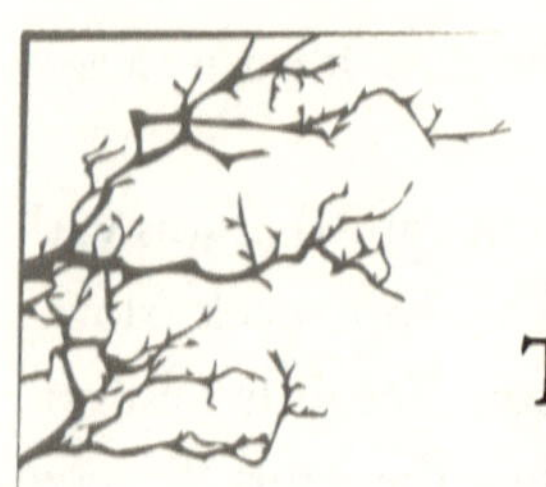

The Library

It was not often that the library I worked at got very busy, but it seemed that when it did everything went wrong with our technology. The ancient printer decided to glitch out and spew its toner all over its insides. The silky powder seemed to get everywhere. Not to mention it ruined several reams of paper. I had enough, I told them we'd either use the office printer or we'd have to replace this one. I would not be using it anymore.

So, I resolved to load it up and cart it off into the basement. The problem, with this plan, was that the old machine was heavy and I wasn't strong enough to cart it down there by myself, so instead, I parked it in an unused room until I'd be able to have a page or one of the directors help me. Which, I still haven't met the new, new board of directors. I swear, these people somehow managed to change almost like clockwork. I looked at the time and realized that I had to get a lot done before we closed or as busy as we'd been I would never get out of there on time.

I stretched my back and got to work on my closing duties. I was honestly super relieved that I wasn't going to be heading down into the unused basement today. After all, the place was a wreck on the best of occasions— dusty, dank, and a pervasive smell of something...else. I've always attributed it to mildew or mold. Not something that I wanted to breathe into my lungs on the pitiful salary that they were able to give me. I shuddered at the thought of medical debt. It was thirty minutes past the end of my shift when I left.

As I started my car I thought, for a brief fleeting second that I had seen something red and bright, like a laser, flashing in the basement window. Maybe it was just the reflection of a stop light or taillights disappearing around the corner. Something mundane, I'm sure. I laughed at my foolishness. Maybe I have been reading too many thrillers lately, they were my favorite comfort read. At least I knew that in my boring mundane life I wouldn't be likely to get caught up in the same situations that the characters in those stories often did.

That night as I went about my nightly routine I found myself thinking about the red laser light in the basement again. The more I thought about it, the more I thought it was a strange thing. There was something...unnerving about it. It was just a stupid laser light of some kind. Probably a neighborhood kid messing around.

With any luck, I'd be able to get someone to help me move that heavy printer downstairs the next day and I would have them help me give the place a once over, just to make sure there isn't someone hiding down there. I flicked on the lamp and picked up my latest read, a Koontz thriller. A bit campy, I suppose, but it was still a fun read.

The next day proved disastrous for getting anything additional done at the library. There was a big meeting and the directors were all tied up in the board room all day, there was a lot of chaos and several of the other library directors from our other branches were coming and going, they all looked elated as they left. As my branch's director left, I asked her what the meetings were about, and she said that the new board has outlined a plan to upgrade and update all of the branches. This was huge, the previous board had been dragging their feet about upgrading anything in our main branch, let alone upgrading all of the branches.

I wondered where they were going to get all of the funding for this project but I wasn't able to dwell on it for more than a few minutes because we got busy again, and then the new board left the office to tour the main branch with my director. I finally got my first good look at them. They were all way, way younger than I was expecting them to be. I supposed, one source of their funding was probably that one of their board members was also a board member at the bank I did my banking at.

They were polite but I wasn't able to commit their names to memory before they headed off to tour the different offices and meeting rooms. They informed me that they were going to spend some time in the basement to walk through all of their big changes for the facility. They were down there for what seemed like a long time. Or maybe I was just bad at tracking time. Either way, they all came out of the basement and then left, maybe it was just my overactive imagination but they all looked...off. Something was different. Maybe they were just tired from a day full of meetings and mental activity. I know that I probably would be a little faded by the end of a busy day like that.

I went about my nightly routine, helping the evening page put books back correctly, I felt like I had to vacuum everything. I made a note in the cleaning log that we were going to need to call in a professional carpet shampooer. I felt like with this new board that the request would be accepted way sooner than it would have been under the previous board. They always seemed to take weeks and weeks to get anything done.

I turned around to go put the vacuum away. I screamed and nearly jumped out of my skin. One of the new board members was standing there, a vague smile crossed his face and then faded. Maybe he felt bad for making me jump as badly as I had. I felt my heart beating in my throat.

"You startled me! I thought everyone else had gone hours ago, I didn't know that you were still here!" I said, suddenly conscious of how squeaky my voice had become during the encounter.

"I am sorry," he said, distantly. "I will be leaving now. I hope you have a good evening."

As he left, I wondered if I was just imagining it but I think he was chuckling. Maybe he was just finally able to laugh once he was sure that I wasn't going to hit him. I don't know, but we had to get our last bit of cleaning done and get out of there, despite knowing for certain that he left I still caught myself looking over my shoulder more than once as I got everything done and left myself.

Over the next couple of weeks, everything became a blur and chaos became the new normal in my sleepy little library. I didn't like it at all. I felt like I was constantly having to move around construction workers and weave through half-finished construction projects that would have probably developed themselves faster than the construction team seemed to be.

One thing that has become something else of a new constant is the presence of the new board. They seemed to always be at our branch. If they weren't tying up the meeting room all day, they were using the basement. She couldn't imagine what they would want to do with the basement. After all, the place was a smelly dank mess. The whole facility seemed like it was just a massive mess lately. I even found a discarded hard hat that was covered in rusty stains. Gross. It sat by my desk hoping that whoever owns it would come by to claim it.

The day carried me away, and I forgot all about the hard hat. It was just another strange occurrence in a day full of them, after all. When I went to lock up my supplies for the evening I realized that the hat was gone. Good, I didn't want it sitting there smelling bad all day, patrons would probably find it another turn-off if the chaos of the building being half-torn apart all of the time didn't turn them off in the first place.

I thought about letting someone on the construction team know about the missing hat in case someone was looking for it and it had been taken by the wrong person but they were all especially frenzied today, from what I had been able to piece together someone involved with the project must have gotten drunk and missed work, but either way he's been out for a couple of days now and nobody seems to know how to get a hold of him. The team said that if they hadn't heard from him or a family by the next day they were going to have to file a missing person report. I didn't know which crew member that they had been talking about but, I can only imagine how much longer the project was going to take to complete now that someone in charge had gone missing.

The board seemed confident that they would be able to complete the project on time anyway, or at the very least that they might have a week or two delays. Nothing dire enough to warrant calling in an extra crew. They wanted to get the upstairs renovations done first and then they would worry about the basement ones, they said those were their biggest plans as they wanted to convert the basement into a series of study rooms and classrooms that could be rented out for different educational opportunities.

I thought it was a great idea that would help generate a lot more income for the library than our current cash flow, so I guess it's a good thing that we have a new board that wants to see all of this come to fruition. Like I said, our old board was so stingy. I hoped that they would be able to continue the growth of our library. The way I see it, it's all just job security for me if they're able to help us with that.

That night as I got ready to pull out of the parking lot, I remembered the flashing laser light. I still hadn't managed to get the printer to the basement. I wondered how hard it would be to borrow one of the construction workers the next day and made a mental note to ask their supervisor if he could spare someone for a few minutes. I wondered if she wouldn't try to donate it somewhere but I figured the directors were all busy with their renovation projects that the last thing they needed to worry about was a printer. If we moved it to the basement it would be out of our way and then they could decide for themselves what we were going to do with it.

The next day, I decided I wasn't going to procrastinate any longer. I found a willing volunteer and we lugged the heavy machine down to the basement. After we got it down there, he was called away but I was able to cart it into a storage room. Curious about what the plans for the renovations were going to be like, I wandered through the rooms looking to see if they'd left anything behind. I didn't see anything and figured I would find out when they were ready when I noticed that a room I hadn't checked was slightly open. From within I caught the faint flicker of red light.

I opened the door and saw that the room had been rearranged. All of the folded tables, chairs, and other things we trotted out once or twice a year had been pushed to the perimeter of the room. In the center of the room was the most peculiar thing. It reminded me of an altar but made as if one had been made out of disassembled furniture. In the center of the altar was a huge red...mass. It was nothing like I had ever seen before.

It was red, welted, and looked...raw. The thing was tall, about five feet in height. The outer layer stretched around itself and slithered back and forth across the meat-colored surface. It reminded me of watching bats fidget their wings in nature documentaries. The worst part about the whole thing was the light that seemed to radiate from within it.

I stepped back, and let out a small gasp. I had no idea what the hell this thing was and I certainly wasn't about to let it get anywhere near me. The thing made a sickening sound, like the soft crunch of bones. With a flurry of sudden movement, it unfurled its wings. As it did so, skeletal remains fell to the floor with a dry sound. This thing enjoyed feeding on people.

Now that the wings were spread wide I could see the thing more clearly and dear god, I wish I hadn't. The creature was essentially a series of mouths stacked on top of one another. The wings were covered in eyes that seemed to blink out of sync with one another. The strange red light was coming from the eyes and seemed to burn their way into my retinas. I felt sick and lightheaded, I felt like that was because of the strange flickering light. It seemed to trash and wiggle, held securely by whatever served as its base, I realized that it couldn't get to me very easily.

I broke the spell first and ran as hard as I could to get away from the thing in the other room. I slammed the door shut behind me and didn't wait to see if it was going to be able to give me chase because I didn't think I'd be able to do much against it, it was feeding on the remains of someone, probably that missing construction worker. There would be more time to dwell on that later.

I had barely made it to the base of the stairs when I felt something hit my mind. That's the only way to describe it. I thought the lights were going dim at first but then I realized that it was my vision that was. I was standing still at the base of the stairs, I wanted to go up to them. Every fiber in my being wanted to, and yet for some reason my body wouldn't respond.

I could feel that strangeness in my mind, it was so hard to describe. It was both cold and alien. It was like I could tell that these thoughts were not my own, that the direction given to my limbs was not my own, but I couldn't stop my body from doing what it was doing. I turned back towards the dark room with its hideous occupant within. I must resist! I must not go! Stop!

I heard a low chuckle in my mind. My struggle was amusing to the thing. I could hear it whisper in a thousand dead languages and yet I knew the words as intimately as my native tongue. It was telling me to be not afraid, that my death would fuel it to greater heights. Mine would be a sacrifice that would bring the world peace. All we had to do was submit to the dark will that infused that cursed flesh.

I don't know how, but I managed to grab a hold of something cold and metal on my way back to the room, it was an outdated fire extinguisher. I wouldn't be needing it for its fire-fighting properties, I just hoped that the gas that powered it was still good because if I was going to be dragged back into that room against my will, I wasn't about to go down without a fight. If the creature could sense my motives it did little to stop me. As I approach the room, I began to feel a new sensation. A hunger. A desire to consume, destroy, and corrupt all that I could get within reach of me.

I knew that these feelings were not my own, but rather the dark intention of that being in the other room. It was feeling triumph and orgiastic joy at the mere thought of all of the horrid things that it would bring to pass against me, against the world, and its ultimate enemy, life.

I stumbled half-conscious into the room. I felt the thing writhing in my mind and at the altar. It was so preoccupied with its victory that it failed to understand the purpose of the fire extinguisher that I held in my hands. I walked up to the creature, repulsed beyond words at the sight of it, of the smell it gave off like burning flesh. Without much, in the way of ceremony, I jammed the nozzle into one of the thing's many mouths. I pulled the pin and squeezed the trigger. I'm sure I missed a few steps in fire safety, but I figured in this case I might be forgiven.

The effect was impressive and nearly instantaneous. Without a means of dislodging the nozzle, the foam and gas had nowhere else to go and instead caused all sorts of unpleasant chain reactions in the creature's hissing, bleeding body. It expanded and froze at nearly the same time, resulting in a momentary and horrific ice sculpture. I smashed it into a thousand pieces with the ice-cold and empty fire extinguisher. With shaky and nerve-dead hands I dropped the canister and numbly left the basement. I've never been back to the library. I don't know exactly what happened but their funding mysteriously ran out, the books were relocated to different branches and that building is now abandoned.

I won't go back there. I've not told anyone else about this experience and I don't think I want to try to relive it yet again. I haven't felt safe in a long time. I'm even packing up to move, I haven't decided where to just yet, but I think once I know I'm safe and away from all of this I'll find someplace new to settle down.

Because I've recently heard a terrifying rumor, nonsense to anyone else but me, it's more than enough of a reason to leave this town and all of the horrible secrets that surely swelter under its surface. That rumor was that sometimes, late at night, if you're driving past the abandoned library, you can see a short red flash of light in the basement window.

The Mummy's Wrath

I work at a small university. We are always growing but it honestly never feels like we're going to be able to keep up with some of the other ones in our area. I fully expect us to get shut down before too much longer. Due to our small size, we don't often get many opportunities to study many ancient artifacts up close very much, let alone anything found in Egypt, those projects usually go to the bigger universities.

As part of a research program, if we were willing to conduct research for the larger project on our own time, they would lend us their artifacts, equipment, and even a full mummy! I fought for weeks to get it approved. This would be an excellent chance to explore non-invasive examinations, something that we don't get often. I had all the paperwork in order and the authorization of the dean. I was even able to secure a couple of grad students to help set up the equipment.

"Doctor, do you have much experience with this sort of work?" one of the grad students asked, I think his name was Eric, who was helping me get the project set up.

"Not nearly enough, but I did take a series of seminars on the latest techniques and I'll be able to reach out to the others in the research project if I find myself in over my head. Could you place the mummy here, in the center? Leave it in the shipping case, I don't want anything to happen to it before we can document it in situ," I told Eric, who along with the other young man whose name escapes me now, began to set the mummy where I had asked them to. They left and I began to test the equipment, following the large manuals that they had included in the mummy's shipping materials. I had no doubt in my mind that these were going to be fun experiments to walk my students through tomorrow, then after my class load for the day, I would be conducting the actual research to submit to the project team. I wish I had an assistant to help me, but the conditions that the dean and the board gave me were strict on our financial budget allowed during the project. If it was going to be mostly pro bono, I would consider myself lucky they were letting me use the facility's electricity.

After making sure that I was satisfied with the equipment I went through the process of taking pictures of the mummy's condition upon arrival to attach to the receipt forms. This was to make sure that if there was a question of damages during shipping or damages during examination they would be able to tell who was the culpable party. I knew the paperwork was going to be endless, I was not, prepared for just how endless it was going to feel. It must have been nearly 8:30 when I left, the security guard, I'll call him Chuck, asked me what I was doing there so late.

"Well Chuck, I get a rare opportunity to examine a real mummy, not just the test ones they send us or the ones that were cats or dogs or what have you. A full, human mummy. It's very exciting for me. I guess that has me pegged as a bit of a nerd, doesn't it?" I asked.

"Not at all doc, I can understand. I might just be a security guard but even I can tell that it's always a good thing when the professor is just as giddy to come to class as some of the freshmen students. Eyes full of wonder, by god it does something good for the soul, sign here and have a safe trip home!" he handed me the form and I scribbled my name on it and left. It did warm my heart to hear something like that. It was a difficult year for most of us that worked at the university with all of the budget cuts that the board had been making, but we were all doing our best to make sure that it wasn't felt by our students and I was positively delighted to know that it was working. I fired up my beat-up old car and let it run for a few minutes before leaving. I noticed that the moon seemed incredibly bright, or maybe it always had been and I just never took the time to notice.

The next day was...Tuesday, we were slotted for our lab time on Wednesday. Despite the full day of lectures that I had, I still wanted to spend time going over everything for the next day. I swiped my key card and let myself into the room. I could have sworn that something was off about the room. So I reviewed my pictures from the previous night.

Oddly enough, everything was in order but I could not figure out why the lid of the sarcophagus was now slightly open. I could have sworn when we left it had been closed. I squinted at the pictures and it was hard to tell if it was or if that was a hint of a shadow. I decided it was probably just my nerves playing games with me.

I shut the sarcophagus lid and laughed at my silly fears. There was no likely explanation for why the lid was like that, and I was only going to drive myself crazy going in circles about it. It was decidedly not a concern as everything was exactly as we had left it. I gave the room one final glance over, content with the placement of everything I shut off the light and closed the door.

I did my usual goodbyes with Chuck and then headed out into the evening air. The moon was big again. Was it always this bright? There was an odd chill coming in the night. I could already see a deep fog attempting to build itself in the low areas between buildings and out in the fields beyond the school grounds. I confess it was the right setting for a horror story.

The short jaunt home felt like it was going to take years. I can't remember when the last time the weather was as foggy as it was tonight. I hoped it would lift early in the morning, I wouldn't want any of my students to miss out on the rare experiments we'll get to do. I let myself into my house and after I did my nightly rituals it didn't take me long to fall asleep. I had the most curious dream that night. I dreamed that I was fumbling my way down a dark hallway. The floor was cold and yet, there was an oddly familiar smell to it. My vision flickered and shook. I guess it reminds me of old televisions when they get bad reception. At one point I was reaching out toward something, but there was something wrong with my arms. They were, covered in bandages?

I could have sworn that I was...I was swaying on my feet and I let out a deep guttural groan. The world began to spin sideways but I was certain that what I was reaching forward toward was a human figure hunched over on the ground. That figure also had a very familiar shape, but I still couldn't quite make out what I was looking at. I just wish that dream me had working eyes. It was very disorientating, the whole thing and it took me several long minutes to collect myself after I jolted awake. The part of the whole dream that seems to be sticking with me so far was the long bandaged arms. There was just something about them that I could have sworn felt more like a memory than a dream.

I didn't get much more sleep before my alarm went off. Now, I don't take much stock in things like omens or dreams that predict the future but there was something...deeply unsettling about this dream that I had. I didn't want to dwell on it, so while I went about my morning routine I did my best to focus on whatever task I was doing so that I might push this dream more firmly from my mind. After all, I had a long day ahead of me and many obligations to fulfill. I wouldn't be doing anyone any favors if I showed up to the day completely unprepared for it.

I even made sure I had enough time to stop by my favorite coffee shop and pick up the latest seasonal blend of coffee that they were showing off. The trip to the school was quiet. There was hardly a soul around. So it felt even more peculiar when I arrived at the school and found that the place was a hotbed of activity and lights. It was like someone had called in every single police officer that they could find in the tri-county area.

I held up my name badge and one of the officers waved me in, I tried to peer around the emergency vehicles to see what was going on and the officer that was in charge of the investigation caught up with me around the same moment.

"Doctor, I think you're the first faculty to arrive. We'll have to ask you to identify the remains," the man said, gesturing for me to follow him. I was already confused, what remains? Had something happened to the mummy? But why all the police? I decided I needed to know what was going on before I went into the building.

"Officer, can you at least tell me what's going on? I don't understand what the deal with the big media circus is out here. If someone bothered the remains unless it was something like a horrible prank gone wrong, this isn't something that we would need all of these police and emergency vehicles for, is it?" I asked, still a little bit in shock by the whole affair. The police officer looked at me with a curious expression on his face and then he shook his head gently.

"You don't have any idea what is going on here, do you? The morning guard arrived to find the guard room empty. There wasn't any sign of the guard. When he came around the security room properly and began to enter the wider hall he realized that there was blood on the floor. There was a lot of blood on the floor," he said. "So he called it in. I don't think you guys are going to be holding any sort of classes today."

"That's awful. So, I what...happened to Chuck?" I asked, mounting horror forming a fresh pit in the bottom of my stomach. I didn't think there would be any room left for another one after seeing all of the lights outside the school.

"I think it would be best if we go inside, looks like one of the deans is just arriving and I think it would save time to explain it to you both at the same time," he waved at the lanky form of John, the admissions dean, who seemed just as confused by the events. "Ah, John? A word?"

Inside the dean's office we heard the events once again as they had been relayed to me, John had been hanging onto every word, his complexion growing paler with each sentence. He sat down heavily in the chair, I couldn't imagine what he was going through. After all, I don't think I've ever had a faculty member's death in the entire time that I've worked here, nearly 8 years in total.

"Has the family been notified? I'll have to reach out to Terry, the guard supervisor, and see if he can help cover things. We're not going to be able to stay open today like this. We'll take the day off out of respect and just shift everything one day over. I know that you're working on a time-sensitive project, if we have a guard that can come in you're welcome to continue your work, if you're able to." he told me.

I was a bit flabbergasted. How could I continue my work knowing that someone has just died in our building? But I also knew that the contract that allowed me to examine the remains was fairly ironclad and that they would not hesitate to cut my opportunities short. I didn't know Chuck all that well, but I think that he would be understanding of the situation that I was in. We didn't even know how it happened or why. As far as we could tell, nothing was taken or missing.

The cameras were reviewed and there was no clear indication of anyone or anything getting into the building. We see Chuck do his rounds, and then everything just went static. When it cleared sometime later Chuck's body was lying in a pool of blood, torn savagely apart. I had a lump in my throat but I needed to get the research done or I would miss the opportunity. As it was, my students were already likely to miss out as the deadline was Friday and it would be shipped out Saturday.

Terry, the guard supervisor was coming to cover the security detail himself. The dean thought about just not having a guard present, but with the materials that we had on loan, he felt that it would be best to have someone else there with him. As he put it, just in case. I wasn't going to complain as I hadn't been looking forward to the idea of having the entire building to myself after everything that has been going on.

The first couple of hours were spent painstakingly photographing everything and verifying the contents of the crates with the artifacts. I also began to take notes on anything that I found, which I would later cross-reference with the notes from the other researchers. This way, anything new would be reviewed and vetted by everyone else in the document chain. It was boring, tiresome work.

Fortunately, I had access to the nearby instructor's lounge which included a fridge where I stored my lunch and all the coffee I would possibly need to get through this experimentation phase. After I did all of the documentation work I could, I went and ate. I was surprised that I was able to eat given how stressful the day had been. Cup of coffee in hand, I returned to the lab.

I stood there for a long moment just appreciating the nature of the mummy. No scientific thoughts, no analysis. Just letting it be for the sake of being. The idea was beautiful and seemed to have health benefits for the community at the time. Among their own deeper religious contexts. I just can't imagine how much respect for the dead they must have had in their daily life, and here I was. Working in the same building that a man had just died in earlier today, like nothing in the world was wrong. Makes you wonder what side of history had it right, after all.

Yet, as I stared at the mummy something was beginning to occur to me. I grabbed my camera and double-checked the photos from the drop-off day and today. There was no way...the mummy appeared...fuller, in today's pictures than it had in the previous ones. I noticed that there was new rust-colored staining on the bandages near the mummy's chest. As I stared at it the shape made sense to me. Bloody fingers grab the bandages as if to open them. The lights went out.

"What the fuck," I said, the room was a ghostly pale blue from the feeble light given off by the camera's LCD screen. I sat the camera down and picked up my cell phone and a moment later had the flashlight turned on. The room was fine, nobody was there with me. I let out a breath in relief. I tried the switch. Nothing. I heard a new sound that I hadn't before because of the ventilation system running. Rain on the roof. It sounded hard. A distant rumble confirmed that a storm must have taken the power out. I shook my head. I have to stop watching so many horror movies.

The university's policy was that in the event of a power outage, all staff members and students are to locate the guard room and remain with the armed security guard until either power is restored, or the deans have authorized them to leave the building. Knowing that they've been under enough financial pressure lately that if I didn't go find Terry they would use it as an excuse to fire me. That was an outcome that I couldn't afford. I stepped out into the hallway and heard the door close behind me. The building was even quieter than before. I almost thought about playing some music, but I couldn't think of any that wouldn't sound ridiculous. I settled for talking out loud, hopefully, that would keep Terry from shooting me if I spook him.

I made it about a third of the way where I was going when I heard something bang behind me. It sounded just like a door, a sound I've heard a million times during my time in education. I knew that I had closed the door behind me. Maybe another professor was working late? I turned and shined the light behind me but all I saw was the faded carpeting and the closed doors of other classrooms.

I let out a sigh. I knew that I was being irrational, but for some reason, I couldn't shake the strange feeling that I wasn't alone. I felt the hair on the back of my neck stand up and every nerve in my body twinged, it was a strange animalistic instinct. I was on high alert. Numbly, I found myself continuing towards the security room at the front of the building. I wanted to laugh at how silly I was being but there was something about the sensation. It didn't feel like this was one of those joke about it moments, this felt very real and I knew what I was feeling for the first time in my entire life. Genuine terror. There was another bang.

I hurried along the darkened hallway, grumbling for the millionth time about the lack of windows and natural lighting. Without the moon or outside lights, this place was almost like a....I laughed, a tomb. It was almost like a tomb. We even had a mummy in ours. At that, I did start laughing and slowed my pace a little to catch my breath. I wouldn't be good for anyone if I had a panic attack.

Somehow, I managed to find my way to the security office in the dark without dying. I did hate the fact that I had to use the stairs, they felt like I was going to be descending into a pit from which I would not be returning. I wouldn't be surprised if after all of this I was going to need to get some therapy. I stopped outside the room marked office and I knocked. There was a sound from within, as the security office was one of the 'inner' offices. A moment later Terry poked his head out, illuminated by a flashlight.

"Ah geez doc, I almost forgot you were here. Nearly gave me a heart attack. Come on in, I've already sent the email and text messages, nobody answered my phone calls so I guess we'll just sit tight until we hear something back, I'll keep this inner door open so we don't suffocate," Terry said, propping the inner door open with a chair.

"Are you expecting anyone else?" I asked him.

"You're the only person on the list as far as I knew. If anyone else is here they're breaking the rules and we know how the bosses feel about that. I'm so worried that I'm going to forget to sign something one time and that'll be the end of it."

"Nah, Terry," I said. "You're the most important part of this whole thing anymore. They couldn't afford to get rid of you, especially...not after...you know..." I said. Terry did know, and didn't feel the need to say anything further about it. As the time passed the air grew staler and staler. Even with the door opened it felt that we might die before anyone gets back to us. We both flinched as heard what sounded like a bang in the distance.

"And you're sure that there isn't anyone else here?" I asked, starting to feel a bit spooked. Terry turned his flashlight back on and checked the paperwork on the desk in front of him. He nodded to himself and with a click turned the light back off.

"It's just us, I'm not sure what that is. Do you think maybe someone left a door or window open? Maybe it's just the ventilation fans kicking in the breeze," he suggested. All of them are perfectly valid explanations and yet none of them provides us any further comfort. There was another bang. Then, a soft peal of thunder. Maybe it was just the storm playing with our heads after all.

We both let out a sigh of relief. Just then the wind kicked up outside and we could feel it howling around the eaves of the building. Even as the wind died down it seemed that mournful moan carried on through the building. I was suddenly reminded of my dream. Hadn't I heard a sound just like that? I softly swore.

"What?" Terry asked.

"Sorry Terry, it's nothing. I just...think I didn't save some of my notes before the power went out. I wonder how much the backup was able to catch before the power went out. I'll have to try to remember them," I lied. The last thing I wanted to do was convince the man with a gun that I was having mummy nightmares while there is a mummy in the building.

Another bang. This time, it had to have been closer. I picked up the phone. I was going to call every one of the deans myself but there was just a click. No service. I tried a couple of different lines and they were all down. I checked my phone and the signal was out.

"Terry, do you have a signal? The phone is out and so is my reception. I don't know how we're supposed to hear from anyone stuck here like this," I grumbled. Terry checked his phone and he was out too, whatever the storm had taken out it was a pretty big chunk of the grid. Terry flipped through the emergency manual but it suggested that they stay put. Naturally.

"If that's someone out there banging doors, I'm going to tell the deans to reprimand them for not paying attention during the safety meetings. After all, we've all been taught that we need to go to the security office, so I'm not sure who the hell they're looking for but my heart can't take much more of it."

"I understand," Terry sighed, I could tell he was probably getting a bit exasperated. I wouldn't envy him in the least if he was. No power, no phones, and no way of knowing how long we're going to be stuck sitting here. I still had to go back and review my notes once the power is back on, otherwise, I'll have wasted the only chance I have to examine the mummy. There was another bang. This time I was sure of it. Whoever it was that was out there banging the doors was getting closer. They would find the office soon, and they would be able to berate them for scaring the two of them half to death. I had half of a mind to tell Terry to get his gun out, so I could shoot them myself. I hated being scared.

Out in the hallway, we heard the low moan echo. I felt the hairs on my neck stand up and then swallowed. Terry shifted uncomfortably next to me. I couldn't see him but I could tell he was wrestling with an idea. He stood up in the darkness.

"I'll have to go see what it is, after all, if someone is hurt I would be the responsible one for not getting them the first aid they might have needed. Stay here, but if you don't hear from me soon please check, uh, just in case I need help," he said, uncertainly. Then taking the flashlight and unclicking his gun holster he stepped out into the hallway.

I wondered how long I was supposed to wait before trying to see if he needed help, but I figured that I was a smart person, I should have been able to figure out what the 'reasonable' amount of time would feel like. I heard him call out to someone in the hallway, ah, so another professor was working late. Mystery solved. Then he called again, this time his voice was more urgent. I started to feel that terror again.

Then I heard a gunshot and flinched. Twice. This was followed by a high scream and then silence. I don't know what was going on out there but I was shaking in my chair. Knowing that I was probably dead either way, I figured I should see if Terry needed my help. I broke the spindly wooden chair n the corner and took the leg with me as a club. It was better than nothing.

I stepped out into the hallway, using the pale blue light of my cell phone flashlight to find my way. I couldn't see anyone standing so I kept my focus on the floor so I didn't trip over anything. I didn't see anyone, but I did hear something odd down an adjacent hallway. As I approached the hallway, there was a darker stain on the carpeting. It was oddly metallic smelling. I knew this was blood.

In the hallway, Terry's body was lying on the floor, slowly being ripped apart by the mummy! He seemed to be digging out organs and tissues and stuffing them inside of his own body. I gagged in revulsion at this horrific display, even as the creature dug out Terry's eyes for his own. As I grew faint and slipped onto the blood-soaked floor I heard the strange shuffling gait, the sound of the fabric against the carpet. My world spun black and I screamed as I fell into nothingness. At the very edge of my senses, I remember feeling a cold hand grip my throat, silencing my scream, and then, nothing more.

About the Author

Tobias Gray lives in southern Michigan with his beautiful wife, way too many pets and a large and joyful extended family that keeps him busy. When he isn't dreaming up reasons to keep himself awake at night, he can be found slaying dragons and putting out fires at one of the local hotel establishments. If you wish to better connect with Tobias, you can do so through the following channels:

Website: https://distantends.net/tobias
Email: tobias@distantends.net
Mastodon: https://writing.exchange/@tobiasgray